1 2 NOV 2018

D0727476

CLAUDIA BOLDT

Harold is unlike any other fox.
His biggest dream is to become a detective.
His biggest love is Swiss cheese.

However, Harold's father has a different plan.
'You'll be a big fox soon, Harold.
It's time you caught a chicken.'

'This will be easy,' thinks Harold.
He knows where lots of chickens live.

Harold snatches one by the legs and runs home,
eager to show his father.

He is nearly home
when the chicken
starts to cluck.

'Bock, bock, bock,
bock, bock, bock,
bock, bock!'

'Why are you clucking?'
Harold asks.
'I don't want to be eaten by a fox!'
cries the chicken.

'I don't eat chickens.
I just have to catch one,'
says Harold.
'I only eat cheese.'

The chicken is confused.
'Don't all foxes eat chickens?'

Harold stops to think.
'If I don't eat chickens, does that mean I'm not a fox?'
In a flash, the chicken is gone.

'Chicken? Where are you?' Harold calls.
'Oh no! What am I going to tell Dad?'

Back home in the den, Harold's father is watching TV.

'Harold, what took you so long? Where's the chicken?'
'It disappeared, Dad.'
'Disappeared?' his father asks.
'You'd better get on the case, Harold.'

The next morning, Harold sets out to search for clues.
He decides to return to the place where he last saw the chicken.

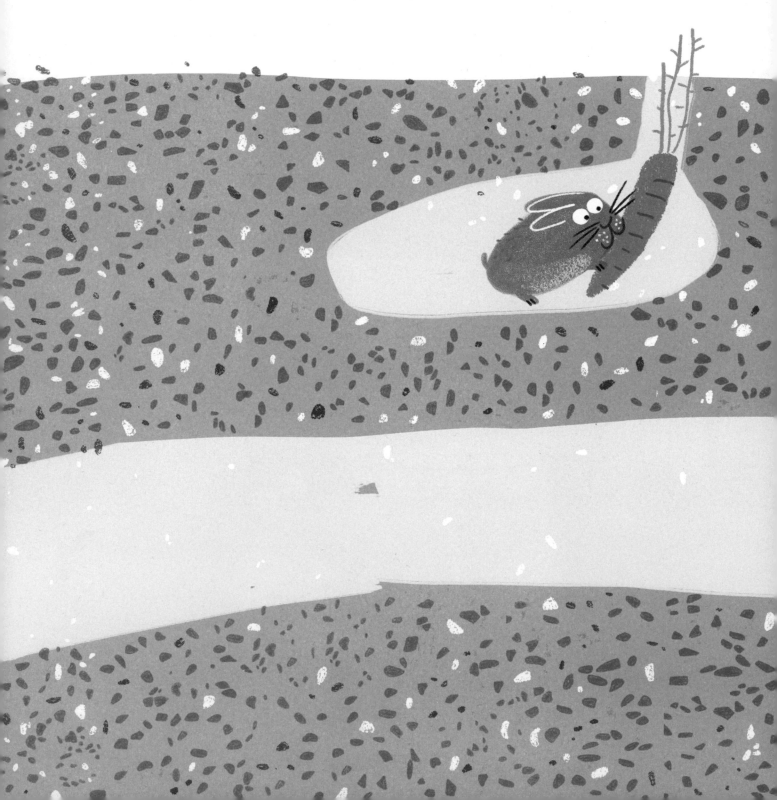

Harold's first clue is a chicken feather.
'This proves the chicken was definitely here.'

Clue number two is eight big paw prints.

'The chicken didn't disappear after all.
It was kidnapped! The question is, by who?'

Harold interviews potential suspects.
'Are these your paw prints?'
'I don't have paws,' replies the boar.

'My paws are too small!' says the raccoon.

'Is this a joke?' asks the mouse.
'Hmmm,' Harold ponders.
'What animal has eight paws,
is bigger than a raccoon, and would
want to steal a chicken?'

'Of course!
An eight-legged,
chicken-eating dinosaur!'
Harold shivers.

Harold knows the only way
to be sure is to follow
the paw prints...

Harold follows the trail as fast as he can —
so fast, he almost misses clue number three.
'I must find that chicken before it gets eaten!'

It's Harold's turn to place an order.

'Can I please have a whole chicken: fresh, not cooked.'

'One Clucking Kebab coming right up!' snarls the wolf.

ROTISSERIE

today's special: chicken stew

Tooth & Claw

When no one is looking,
Harold unwraps the chicken ...

... and takes off with it!

'Hey! You need to pay for that!' shouts the wolf.
'That's my donkey!' yells the farmer.

Back home, Harold shows his father the chicken feather.
'I solved the mystery, Dad! Two wolves stole
my chicken. But don't worry, I got it back.'
'You outfoxed two wolves and ate the chicken?!
That's my boy! You're a big fox now.'

But little does Harold's father know ...

... the chicken is long gone.

Other titles available:

First published 2015 by order of the Tate Trustees by Tate Publishing,
a division of Tate Enterprises Ltd, Millbank, London SW1P 4RG
www.tate.org.uk/publishing
This paperback edition published 2018
Text and Illustrations © Claudia Boldt 2018. All rights reserved.
A catalogue record for this book is available from the British Library.
ISBN 978-1-84976-603-6
Distributed in the United States and Canada by ABRAMS, New York.
Library of Congress Control Number applied for.
Printed in China by Toppan Leefung Printing Ltd.